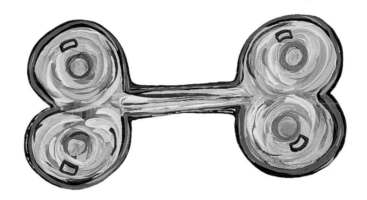

HAPPY DOG!

LISA GRUBB

PHILOMEL BOOKS

Jack Cat was happy.
It was Saturday,
his favorite day of the week.

But when he looked outside,

he saw rain pouring down.

"Oh, no!" he said.

"I want to go play with my friends.

Now I'll be all alone.

Unless . . . Wait, I know what to do!

"A new friend! I'll call him Happy Dog."

"Oh, boy," Happy Dog shouted.

"Puddles! I LOVE to splash in puddles."

"Happy Dog, wait!" said Jack Cat.

"Your paint isn't dry yet!"

But Happy Dog was too excited to wait.

Happy Dog ran
to the biggest puddle
he could find
and jumped in.

SPLASH!

But when he looked down,

he saw the puddle had changed color.

"Oh, no," he said,

"my paint is washing off in the rain!"

Luckily, Jack Cat knew just what to do.

"There! As good as new," said Jack Cat.

"Now, no more playing outside until the rain stops."

"What should we play with inside?"
Jack Cat asked.

Happy Dog had a wonderful idea.

"Follow me!" he said.

They began to paint,
and the rainy day
outside disappeared.
They painted a giant castle
made of Swiss cheese.
Happy Dog was king.

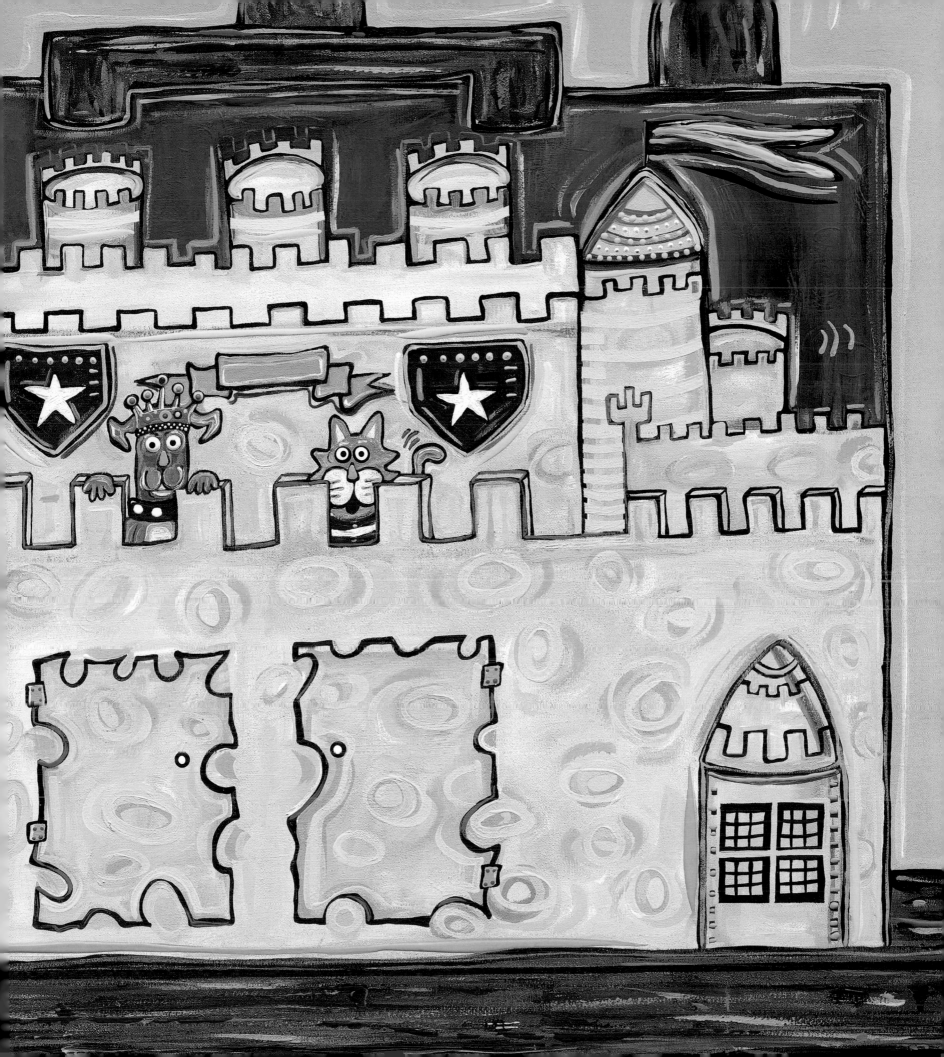

Then they painted a starship
and rode to the moon.

And a big, red fire engine with a bell.

Jack Cat was captain of the fire department.

Happy Dog grew sleepy, and needed a nap.

So Jack Cat painted him

a big field of flowers to lie down in.

When he was done, he felt sleepy too.

"I love Saturdays," Jack Cat said
as he curled up with his pillow.
"They're my favorite day of the week."

Special thanks to
Amanda, Curtis, Billie, Deborah,
and my editor, Michael Green,
for believing in my art.

PHILOMEL BOOKS
a division of Penguin Putnam Books for Young Readers,
345 Hudson Street, New York, NY 10014.
Philomel Books, Reg. U.S. Pat. & Tm. Off.
Published simultaneously in Canada.
Manufactured in China by South China Printing Co. Ltd.
Design by Carolyn T. Fucile.
The text is set in Badger Medium.
The art for this book was created with acrylic paint on canvas.
Library of Congress Cataloging-in-Publication Data
Grubb, Lisa. Happy Dog! / Lisa Grubb. — 1st Impression.
p. cm. Summary: On a rainy Saturday, Jack Cat creates a new friend
by painting a dog and then together they paint new adventures for themselves.
[1. Painting — Fiction. 2. Rain and rainfall — Fiction.
3. Cats — Fiction. 4. Dogs — Fiction.] 1. Title.
PZ7.G93184 Hap 2003 [E] — dc21 2002010986
ISBN 0-399-23707-0
1 3 5 7 9 10 8 6 4 2
First Impression